Written and illustrated by
David McPhail

Harcourt, Inc.

San Diego   New York   London

Requests for permission to make copies of any part of the work should be mailed to the following address: Permissions Department, Harcourt, Inc., 6277 Sea Harbor Drive, Orlando, Florida 32887-6777.

www.HarcourtBooks.com

First published in 1984

For the inspiration for page 9, my daughter Jaime and I would like to thank Irene Haas for her wonderful book *The Little Moon Theater*, a Margaret K. McElderry Book, published by Atheneum, 1981.

Illustrations colored by John O'Connor

Library of Congress Cataloging-in-Publication Data
McPhail, David M.
Sisters/written and illustrated by David McPhail.
p. cm.
Summary: Although two sisters are different in many ways, they are alike too—most importantly, in their love for each other.
[1. Sisters—Fiction.] I. Title.
PZ7.M2427Si 2003
[E]—dc21   2002003755
ISBN 0-15-204659-3

O Q R P N

Manufactured in China

The illustrations in this book were done in pen and ink and hand colored with watercolors.
The display type was set in Kennerley Old Style.
The text type was set in Kennerley Old Style.
Color separations by Bright Arts Ltd., Hong Kong
Manufactured by South China Printing Company, Ltd., China
This book was printed on totally chlorine-free Enso Stora Matte paper.
Production supervision by Sandra Grebenar and Pascha Gerlinger
Designed by Barry Age

For Sandy and Lisa
and
Gabrian and Jaime

This is the story of two sisters…

who, in many ways, were different.

One was big.

One was little.

One liked to wear
two different colored socks.

One didn't like to wear socks
(or shoes) at all.

One liked baseball.

The other found it boring.

One's favorite food was pizza.

The other preferred corn on the cob.
(She called it "cob on the corn.")

One sister was crazy about frogs...

…the other wasn't.

One liked to get up with the sun.

The other would sleep all day.

One liked to chase fireflies through
the grass...

while the other liked to lie back and
look at the stars.

The two sisters were alike
in many ways, too.

They both liked horses…

…and sugar-snap peas
fresh from the garden.

Both sisters liked to
help bake cookies…

...and to play in puddles.

And a pile of leaves was never safe
with those sisters around.

They both liked to draw…

and to skate.

And dancing was something
neither sister could live without.

They fought over the piano…

…and made up over tea.

And both felt the day would not be
complete without a swing after supper.

But the way they were most alike
was the most special way of all.

Because, you see,
they loved each other so very much.